65 MILES

Jill Faith Camlin

bean dog productions
in association with

DORRANCE PUBLISHING CO., INC.
PITTSBURGH, PENNSYLVANIA 15222

All Rights Reserved
Copyright © 1998 by Jill Faith Camlin
No part of this book may be reproduced or transmitted
in any form or by any means, electronic or mechanical,
including photocopying, recording, or by any information
storage and retrieval system without permission in
writing from the publisher.

ISBN # 0-8059-4414-1
Printed in the United States of America

First Printing

For information or to order additional books, please write:
Dorrance Publishing Co., Inc.
643 Smithfield Street
Pittsburgh, Pennsylvania 15222
U.S.A.
Or visit our web site and on-line catalog at *www.dorrancepublishing.com*.

This story is for my dad and my pop,
two men who taught me to walk tall.

...the testing of your faith develops perseverance.
Perseverance must finish its work so that you may be mature
and complete, not lacking anything.

NIV
James 1:3-4

I look back on that night, five years ago; it was the
longest and hardest night of my life. I would never want to live it
again. But it was also the best night of my life.
The only one I am proud of.

It was just me and Adam and 65 miles.
Down that long road all we found was misery, the break-you-down
kind that makes you want to sink to your knees and just give up.
But we stuck together and we got through it all right.
Well, truthfully, God got us through. Thank you, God.

But me and Adam, we sure did stick together.

1

The sun was sinking like a bloody line drive in left field. It was still warm out, still short sleeve weather, but it was early May and the nights were unpredictable.

We cut through the bramble and stumbled out onto the fading asphalt of Walmart's parking lot. Little prickle balls clung to our pant legs and shoe laces. The lot seemed long and empty like an open prairie. We were in Berea, Kentucky, and that's how things were there, long and empty.

"Life in the fast lane or to hell with the fast lane?"

Adam knotted his brow, then smiled, "To hell with it!"

I smiled, too. "To hell with it" was one of those lines that just felt good to say and it felt good to hear.

"Forgive and forget or revenge is a dish best served cold?"

I puckered my lips. "Um, forgive, but never forget."

"Sorry, Jill, not one of the choices."

That's me, by the way, Jill. Sorry, I was never big on formal introductions. I could sit next to you on a Greyhound bus and talk your ear off all the way across the country, never once mentioning my name or asking for yours.

"I made this game up. You get one of those."

"One of what? A cheat?"

"It's not a cheat. It's an ad-lib. You get one ad-lib in case you got a conflict of interests. I strongly believe in forgiving, but don't you ever forget. If you forget all the blues you been through, what was the point in singing them? See? So, I got to answer with forgive, yeah, but never forget."

I loved talking to Adam cause I could talk intelligently to him and best of all, he could talk intelligently back. That's a rare commodity these days.

"Well, awright." Adam had a born and bred Kentucky drawl. "Now, what about a pass? Can I choose not to answer and just flat out pass?"

"Why would you do that? If you choose not to answer and just pass that would be covered under the ad-lib policy."

"Naw. An ad-lib is coming up with an answer right on the spot, where's the pass is choosing not to give an answer at all. There's an awful big difference."

"Yeah, yeah, all right. You get one pass and one ad-lib."

"What about time outs? You get any of those?"

"No. No time outs. Fall of an empire or rise of a new regime?"

"Well, come on, now." Adam kicked a rock. It skipped up off the lot and dinged an old pick-up truck. There were a lot of pick-up trucks in Kentucky and a lot of bearded dudes in ball caps who drove them around. "People remember the fall not the rise. Tell me, who rose up after the Romans?"

"Like you know."

"Come on."

"Outside of Strikes Back and States Building, how many empires can you name?"

"The Ottomans, dammit."

"Oh, yeah. Huh. I forgot all about the Ottomans. They beat the Romans?"

"Nuh."

"So who beat the Romans?"

Adam shrugged. "Coulda been the Turks."

"The Turks?"

"Yeah."

"No."

"What'd you got against the Turks?"

"They're the Turks, not the Hoosiers."

"Yeah," he said. "So they'd be definite underdogs."

"We're talking the Romans. Going away, the greatest empire of all time. Spread would be at least fourteen."

Adam stopped at the curb and shoved his hand deep into his pocket. "You wanna bet on this?"

"Turks/Romans, Romans giving fourteen?"

"I'll take ten. You're seriously under estimating the power of the Turks."

"Will you stop digging in your pockets like you're going to find some money."

"Hey, I got a little change."

I stood in front of the rumbling, green soda machine. "How much you got?"

He took inventory of his palm. One dime, three pennies, lint fuzzies, and a toe nail. "Thirteen cents."

"And a toe nail."

"Yeah."

"Don't forget the toe nail."

"Yeah, awright, awready, how much you got?"

"Not much. More than thirteen, less than a buck." I slung my pack off my shoulder. It was an old bag I had carried with me since the sixth grade. That bag had a lot of sentimental value to me. Almost as much as my leather jacket.

"Aren't you hot?"

"What? The jacket?"

"Yeah."

"Nuh. This jacket breathes. It's my second skin." Rain or shine, in the cold dead of winter or the hot heart of summer, I was faithful to that jacket like a good woman to her man. "You shoulda brought a jacket."

"It's seventy degrees out."
"Now it is."
"How much you have there?"
"Sixty-three," I said.
"Thirteen and sixty-three. What's that?"
"Eighty-six."
"Seventy-six."
"You sure?"
Adam nodded. "Sixty-three and ten."
"Seventy-three."
"And three."
"Yeah, you're sure. See, I was figuring in the retail value of your toe nail."

He totally ignored me and that made me laugh.

He continued to ignore me. "Wanna get three pops?"

"Machine doesn't take pennies. Feel like running in and trading for a nickel?"

"Naw. Two's good."

"It's a long walk to your house. Think two's enough?"

"If I have to run in, then two's plenty." Adam fed the machine the change and pounded the bar that read Green Lightning.

The insides of the machine growled like a mechanical stomach ache and belched out the can of soda.

"What's your pleasure?" He asked me.

"Get me one of those, too."

"You know," Adam said as he slipped the machine more change, "Jesus could feed the five thousand with two cans of Green Lightning."

"Yeah. He was a pretty resourceful guy."

Adam stood up with a can of cheap lemon lime in each hand, like a school boy ready to clap the chalkboard erasers. We looked at each other for a beat.

"Welp," I said.

"Welp."

"We could still turn back."

"And do what?"

"I don't know. Go back to campus, just hang out, like always. We got visitation tonight. You could come up to my room, we'll watch *Glory* again."

Glory, in my opinion, is the greatest movie ever made. Adam thought pretty high of it too, he had watched it with me on twelve different occasions. But *Blade Runner* was his favorite.

"Jill, ten minutes ago this was the best idea you had heard all semester. Now you want to turn back?"

"I want you to be sure. If we're going, we're going 65 miles. That's a long trip. Especially when you ain't wearing your Nikes."

He looked down at his feet. Hiking boots. "Hey, now. These here are professional hiking boots."

I stand corrected. Professional hiking boots.

"Rock climbers on ESPN 2 wear these. Top of the line, honey."

"Oh yeah?"

We blinked at each other.

"So. What do you want to do?"

He sighed. "I want to get away from here for a while. I want to forget college and just go. That whole scene, it's digging up my ass like a gopher and starting to pull. Me and you, Jill. The two of us, just walking and talking things out. It'll be good."

"Yeah. We all ready got the soda, right?"

He grinned and clinked the cans. "We can't turn back now."

"All right then. Let's go to your house."

"Let's go."

So that's how we got into the mess, by wanting to get away and just leave all our troubles behind at Berea. It wasn't that Berea was a bad place, we had it real good there. But Gilligan's Isle was probably paradise for the first month. Without a motor car or a single luxury, the castaways built bamboo rafts and transistors out of coconuts.

Berea was our little Gilligan's Isle. Only we didn't have to wait to be rescued. All we had to do was walk.

2

Berea College had a beautiful campus. In the fall the trees were on fire with crisp autumn colors and the sun blazed down in orange glory behind the old Berean Baptist Church.

In the winter the snow came and clung to the trees and the old brick buildings and left the campus sleeping under a cold blanket of peaceful loneliness.

In the springtime the air was sweet and clean and shouts of laughter and the aluminum ping of a softball bat road on it for a country mile.

In the summer the grass bled green and the kids tossed Frisbees out on the quad and made love down by the tennis courts under the big, fat moon and a million stars.

Berea College, to put it plain and simple, is a great place. Every student who enrolls gets a full scholarship. It's a private school, so that scholarship kind of works as a twenty thousand dollar coupon every year.

Every student is required to work on the campus at least fifteen hours a week in return. I signed on as a waitress at Boone Tavern, a southern style restaurant owned by the college. It was real world work, no joke, a lot of hop and hustle. There was a no tipping policy, so some nights it felt as if I was breaking my back for nothing. But if I stopped to think about it and broke that scholarship down by the hour, well, I was on the big fat side of a good deal. Sometimes I wonder if I hadn't messed things up so bad, how far I could've gotten with the golden opportunity Berea offered me.

Anyhow, Adam, he earned his keep working in the Art building. I'm not sure what he was supposed to be doing over there. I visited him a couple of times while he was on the clock and he just sat behind a desk and collected student I.D.s and ate pizza-flavored Combos he'd get out of the snack machine.

Adam was a little hairy guy. He had black tufts sprouting on his toes and knuckles and I assume in other hair related regions, too, but I never saw him with his shirt off or his pants for that matter. He had a little bit of a gut on him, but he wasn't fat. I mean, if he started doing jumping jacks his belly wouldn't jiggle or nothing.

He had a thick, shaggy head of hair and a full biker's beard going for him. There was a dangerous look about him, the kind of look that made you avoid eye contact and cross to the other side of the street if you seen him coming.

One time the two of us went into a Save-A-Lot cause it was that bloody time of the month for me and I was fiending like an addict for a box of Milk Duds. Adam had his head wrapped tight in a dark bandana and his hands buried deep in a long, black trenchcoat. The store security guard tailed us from aisle to aisle, giving us a suspicious eye, while he whistled and pretended he wasn't tailing us.

To the naked eye, Adam was a drifter. A man not to be trusted with a big coat and opened shelves of merchandise. But I knew Adam pretty damn good. And I'll tell you what, there was no soul alive that I trusted more. He was the best friend I ever had in my entire life.

We were walking the shoulder of Route 15 and we'd be walking that road until we ran out of horizon. So Adam decided to start a conversation.

"You heard from Brian yet?"

The bottom dropped right out of my heart when he mentioned that name.

"Nope," I said. "Two weeks. The boy's known for two weeks and nothing. He's got me pacing like a convict in my little cell, staring at the phone, like if I hope hard enough, it'll ring."

He didn't say anything.

"He's got me sick inside, Adam."

"You sure you want to keep it?"

"Yeah, I'm sure. What do you think I am? Chicken?"

"What about your mom? You mention it to her yet?"

"Nuh. I don't got the heart to be breaking her heart just yet. You and Bri, you's are the only two I've told. And Bri, who knows, he coulda left the country by now."

My period had been late. So I made an appointment at the women's health clinic downtown. I walked in, peed in a cup, and then came out six weeks pregnant.

We walked ten paces with just the gravel under our feet doing the talking.

"Hey, Adam?"

"Huh?"

"This walk's a good idea."

3

Daylight was gasping its last breath, scorching the evening sky with orange and red.

"Hot damn, now there's a beauty." Adam hustled off into the brush. He bent down and I heard his knees pop. He picked up a twisted walking stick. He hopped up and paraded around, twirling the stick like Charlie Chaplin.

"How do I look?"

I had to admit. "You carry wood well for a shorter guy."

"Thank you."

Across the road was a cow pasture. It was marked off with a long run of wired fencing.

"Hey. I thought cows slept standing up."

Adam joined my side again. "I think they do."

"Well, look at that one." I pointed to a fat black and white. It laid on the ground with its front legs tucked under her. She blinked at us while she chewed cud and contemplated the meaning of life.

"She's not sleeping."

"No," I agreed. "But she's lying down. If cows can lie down, then why do they sleep standing up? It's got to be more comfortable sleeping lying down than standing up, right?"

"Welp." He said that real slow, like he was getting set to use his ad–lib. "Maybe sleeping standing up's a defense mechanism. When they're lying down and wide awake they're aware of what's going on around them. But when they're asleep, danger can sneak up on them from all sides. So, they sleep standing up to make that potential danger believe they're really awake."

"What about cow tipping?"

"What about cow tipping?"

"You ever hear of cow tipping?"

"Of course I heard of cow tipping. When you sneak up on a cow sleeping standing up, knock her over, then run for the hills."

"That's a pretty crappy defense mechanism."

"It doesn't take a genius to figure out cows ain't geniuses."

"Look at all of them. Just watching us."

The cows stood there, perfectly still except for their chewing jaws. Their eyes followed us like the evil eyes in a haunted house portrait.

Adam shuddered. "Creepy. Every single one of them's eyeing us hard."

"Cause we're different. Two white kids walking through an all cow neighborhood. You feel that?"

"What?"

"The heat between us and them. Speciel-tension."

"Speciel-what?"

"Tension. Mistrust between the species. They don't trust us cause we fatten them up, lop off their heads, and eat them."

"And knock them over when they're trying to sleep."

"Exactly. " I said. "And we don't trust them cause they're 500 pounds of living rawhide and rump roast. If cows wanted to, they could rule the earth."

"Naw. If it came down to a war between the species, based on sheer size, the elephants would win out."

"Elephants can't rule."

Adam frowned. "They could do just as good a job as your cows."

"The blue whales would beat them in the great speciel war."

"Whales are in the water. They could be the single great water power, I'll give you that, but their jurisdiction would end at the shoreline."

"So nothing beats the elephant?"

He threw up his hands to state the obvious. "Whose gonna beat the elephant?"

The conversation got more ridiculous. I went on to propose a theory that the blue whales could align themselves with the nation of field mice and take over the land too, but Adam disagreed. We went on with that for another 4 miles. I'll spare you the details.

4

I'm no where near beautiful. But I got a cute smile and a big butt. That gets me a little bit of male attention, especially from foreigners and black guys. This concerns my grandmother a great deal.

"Jill," she's always saying, "you don't want no blackie. They don't know how to treat a woman right. It just isn't in their blood."

Then she'll follow that up with: "Now, I have a lot of black friends, so I know how their culture is and trust me, because I love ya, you don't want no blackie."

She warned me about the dagos, the spics, the japs, and the Jews, too, because she knew their cultures and she loved me.

I don't know. I just played with the hand that the good Lord dealt me. I kept my love life so secret from my grandmother she feared I was a lesbian.

"You like boys, don't ya, Jill?" she once asked me while me, her, and my grandpop played cards.

I looked at her to see if she was serious. She was. "Yeah, Gram."

"Oh, thank God. I worry about you." She said as she threw the queen of hearts. "I'm only asking because I love ya."

"I know, Gram. I know."

It was because she loved me so much that I decided I would wait until she passed on or went senile before I settled down and tied the knot.

I had been hustling tables when I met Brian. He sat alone in the table by the window. I went over with my pen and pad in hand. "Good afternoon."

He turned from the window real slow, like he had all the time in the world and laid his big brown eyes on mine. He was tall and handsome and my grandmother would've never had him over for Christmas dinner. An easy grin spread smooth over his face and I could feel my insides get hot and queasy.

"How you doin, girl?" His voice sealed it. It was deep and lazy and made me want to hear him recite the alphabet a hundred times over. I was going to be in love with this guy, I knew it right there, before I even took his drink order.

"Are you ready or," I fumbled with my pad, "do you need more time?"

He licked his lips. "I'm ready, baby. Are you?"

I was still gazing at his lips. "Huh?"

"Are you?"

"Yeah, yeah." I blinked out of it. "I mean if you're ready then I'm ready."

"Well, I'm ready." He wouldn't stop looking at me and I couldn't stop looking at him.

"Okay," I swallowed a dry lump. "What would you like to order?"

"Candle light and a table for two."

I was a downright sucker for a confident grin and a Hollywood line. "Why don't you join me, girl?"

"I can't."

"You got a boyfriend or something?"

"No!" I spit that word out of my mouth like it was black licorice. "I'd love to join you, but I'm sorta working right now."

"What time you get off?"

"Seven."

He stood to leave. I was looking him dead in his broad chest. "I'll see you at seven o'clock then."

"Aren't you here to get something to eat?"

He brushed my cheek with his strong hand and my heart started spinning like a coin on a table top. "I don't want to spoil my appetite for tonight."

He left me speechless, standing alone in that window, watching him go. I couldn't help but notice he had the juicy tight end of a tight end.

Brian had been man enough to put the biggest decision of my entire life in my belly, but it had been a long two weeks since I last heard from him.

I was mad at him for not coming to see me after I had given him the news. I guess he was scared and needed time to think. But I was scared too, dammit, and I needed him.

5

Adam needed to find direction and I needed to find a whole lot of courage, so we were walking 65 miles to Mount Sterling, a crusty little town that had neither. Instead it had all night liquor stores and trailer parks. But it was the place that Adam called home and to me, being from Jersey, it was a home away from home. So home was where we were headed.

Adam's father was a big man with a ripe, round gut and a square head. He wasn't much for conversation. He spoke only in commands. The first time I ever met him he grimaced at me like he had intestinal gas and said, "Sit down. Make yourself comfortable. Adam, get her a cold pop to drink." Then he went back to the fishing show he had been watching.

He was a man concerned about his beer getting warm and what time dinner would be ready. He was a cop and he was awful proud of the squad car parked in his driveway for all the neighbors to see and respect.

Adam's mother was the perfect compliment to his father, which is to say she didn't say much and she did as she was told. She was plump and small and always smiling. She always had trouble with the electric can opener and always needed help twisting the lid off the applesauce jar. Her eyebrows were plucked so fine and thin she padded through life with a constant look of surprise on her face.

Adam wasn't happy at college and he didn't miss home. Sure, he loved his parents, but he did not miss either of them. He didn't like where he was and he didn't miss where he had come from. He was lost and the only direction to go, if he had the guts, was straight ahead into the unknown.

"Hey, what'd your pop say when you told him about the New Orleans plan?"

"Oh, man!" He shook his head. "I didn't know Pop had so many veins in his head. When I said I was thinking about dropping out of school and moving down there, all of them jumped out at once and started throbbing something ugly."

"So what're you gonna do?"

He shrugged. "I dunno. It's getting cold out here, though. I shoulda brought a jacket."

For real, I'm not the kind of kid to say "I told you so." So I didn't. I just stripped out of the jacket and gave it to him.

"No, you'll be cold."

"Only for a little while. We'll take turns."

He thought about it, thought about being macho and strong and braving the elements, but I guess he would have rather been warm cause he took the jacket from me.

"College is awright cause I don't have to live at home listening to Mom and Pop gripe about how I'm not in school and how I'm wasting my life. But when I'm at school, I'd rather be laying around back home in my underwear and socks telling Mom and Pop to just get off my back. It's a rock and a hard place, really. College ain't where I belong, Jill. I know that. But I got no better place to be."

"Quit."

"Pop would shave my balls off with a potato peeler. Naw, I can't quit. I'd rather be plum miserable than dead."

"You don't have to be miserable."

"As long as my Pop draws breath and drinks beer, yeah, trust me, I do."

It was nearing nine o'clock. We had followed Route 15 till it ran out of heart and became Main Street. Main Street was full of gutter trash and lit by bar signs. It cut like a rusty knife through Richmond, a railroad town with seedy Irish pubs on every block. There was O'Bannon's, O'Sullivan's, O'Reilly's, and O'Rourke's. The Wednesday night party crew gathered on the street corners, moving from bar to bar with the hopes of finding a good time they'd never remember the next morning.

One thing I've learned in life is never provoke a drunk man into conversation. Don't ask him for the time, don't say, "how you doing," don't tell him his hat is on fire. Just keep your head down, your feet moving, and your mouth shut.

That's how me and Adam approached the situation in front of O'Malley's. There were two college chicks in short skirts leaning on Daddy's Mustang. Entertaining them were three big dudes with beer on their breath and asshole on the brain.

As soon as we walked on by, their conversation dried up like pigeon stool on a park bench. Their eyes were on us, I could fell them eating through the back of my head. Then the shadow fell long and dark across the sidewalk.

"Look, y'all. Davey Crocket and his bitch're exploring for the fountain of youth."

Just keep on walking, I thought.

"Hey, Crocket. I'ma talking to you."

Just keep on walking, I thought.

"Yo, Crocket. Me and the fellas're one bitch short. You mind if we borrow yours?"

Just turn around and give them hell, I thought.

I wheeled on my heels. "You got a fat mouth, Andy Capp."

That drunk grin skittered off his horse face in a hurry. He stood there blinking at me, with a brown long neck in one hand and a belt loop in the other.

All this fire burned up in my gut. Brian had told me once that it'd be me and him against the world, but when the bell rung, he had left me to fight alone. I didn't need this lit loser laughing at me. Not tonight. I was in a fighting mood and if Capp was drunk enough to call my bluff, why he'd find out I wasn't bluffing.

"I got a lot of stuff on my mind and the last thing I need is you on my nerves."

"Hey, Crocket. You best tell that bitch of yours she's 'bout to get you killed."

Adam took me by the elbow. "Jill, come on. This guy's a fruit loop."

"I'm picking the fight with you, Capp." I pulled free of Adam. "Crocket ain't got nothing to do with this."

Adam whispered, "Jill, what're you, nuts?"

"Bitch, you are nuts!"

I slung my pack to the ground and stepped out of his shadow. "At least I got them, Capp."

He glared at me. His eyes shrunk and burned like smoldering hot coals. I could see his soul was full of hate. But I was full of a force far more dangerous. Fear.

Adam had me by the elbow again. "Jill, this guy's Goliath."

Adam might of had a point. But he was a drunk Goliath at best. I was a long shot, even I knew that, but I was a long shot fighting to get my life back. Plus, I wasn't walking into this ugly mess empty handed.

"Gimme the stick, Adam."

"What?"

"The stick." I snatched the wood from him.

"You're really gonna fight this goon?"

I turned to him. "Yeah, I'm gonna fight!" I was talking about a lot more than this crazy confrontation.

He bit his lower lip and nodded. If I was going to fight, then dammit, Adam was going to fight too. He stripped out of the jacket and let it fall at his feet.

Now, the two of us weren't exactly Batman and Robin. Adam was more like Gandhi, except he never fasted. And I only had one fist fight in my whole life, back in the second grade over a kickball game with a kid named Oko Robinson. But the two of us were going into battle together. And if we died under the flickering banners of Budweiser and Red Dog, why we were going to die together.

I held our walking stick before me like an ancient saber. Adam held his dukes up in front of his snarl like a guy who'd never held his dukes up in his life.

"Crocket, don't come exploring my street corner," Capp warned in between hiccups. "There ain't no pot of gold at the end of this rainbow. Only a world of hurt."

Me and Adam swaggered like a pair of gunslingers right into the world of hurt.

Capp glanced back at his posse, but they didn't draw their six guns and stand by his side. Instead, they all climbed into that Mustang and looked awful ready to crank the ignition and ride off into the sunset.

"Crocket, you stupid little hick. You best wise up right quick or I'ma gut your dumb ass." Capp shifted on his feet.

We kept coming.

Capp smashed his beer bottle on the Mustang's hood.

"Dammit, John, this is my Daddy's car," the blond chick cried.

"Shut yer mouth, woman. I'ma bout to crack some skull."

"My Daddy'll crack yer skull if you done put a dent in his car."

Capp snapped. "Shut the hell up, bitch. I'm busy, dammit."

We had closed the gap. The showdown was now a stand off.

Capp towered over us, his red eyes swam in watery rage. His one hand was shaking bad, his other swayed the jagged bottle at us like it was a talisman and would keep us at bay.

"Don't fuck with me, Crocket. I swear I'll cut your heart out."

Somewhere during the conflict Adam swapped Gandhi's sack cloth for a shiny set of brass balls. "Oh, we're gonna fuck with you, Capp," he scowled. "We're gonna fuck you so fucking hard you won't fucking fuck no more."

Maybe it was all the fucks flying around my head like mad men, maybe it was Adam all of a sudden turning into Al Capone, or maybe it was the fact that I saw Brian's face on this drunk prick instead of his own, I don't know, but I totally lost my cool.

The stick burned in my hands and pumped my arms full of vengeance. I swung that stick with all my might. Swung it clean and level and true like my dad had taught me. I caught Goliath square on his jaw like his head had been a 3–2 breaking ball.

CRACK!

Goliath rocked up off his feet and bounded on the middle of the Mustang's hood. His gigantic bulk dented the car with a hollow thump and then he rolled off the front end, into the street. He was laid out like a snow angel, the busted beer bottle still clenched in his fist.

His posse stood up on the leather upholstery and looked down on their sprawled leader. He didn't make any move to get up. He just laid flat on his back, admiring the Big Dipper.

They looked at us next. I'll tell you what, they had sobered up real quick.

"What if he's dead?" the blond chick asked me.

I looked at Capp. In my high school days I had never really been a power hitter. I usually singled or worked a walk. There was no way I could've knocked Capp's life clear over the left field fence. He'd be coming to in about ten minutes.

Adam shrugged at her. "More beer for you."

Then me and Adam turned away and headed for Mount Sterling once again.

6

My dad died six years ago. Cancer got him. They tried chemo, but the radiation couldn't stop the disease. It ate him up one day at a time and stole him out of my life a week before my high school graduation.

Death is the toughest thing to deal with, especially when you ain't the one doing the dying. There's a sense of peace in seeing the sweet chariots coming forth, in knowing your suffering will all be over soon. I could see this in my dad's eyes.

But when you're left behind, when all you got left of your dad's a soul full of memories and a gray slab of concrete at the head of the grave, life ain't life no more. It's a deep ache that never lets you forget the man you took for granted.

I loved my dad. God blessed me with a great father. My dad would come out to most every softball game I played and when the game was far away at a different school, he'd always be waiting on me under the humming light of the lot, when our team bus turned the corner home.

My dad helped me write a report on Texas when I was in the fifth grade, and our project about the Barnegat Bay won third place at the eighth grade science fair. My dad carried me in his arms into the emergency room when I was twelve, and I squeezed his hand tight while the doc sewed up my leg with fourteen stitches.

I never had a hero growing up. I read comic books and traded baseball cards and watched the cowboys in the Saturday Afternoon Matinee every week, but none of those guys were ever real to me. None of those guys ever picked me up after I lost a big game or helped me study my school books or let me bleed on them after I fell off a ladder. None of those guys were my dad.

But my dad, he was never my hero. A hero's a guy who rises to the occasion and is great for one fleeting moment. My dad was there for me every time I needed him. My dad was my dad. God, I miss him.

7

What I did to Andy Capp that night I can't take back. But I sure am sorry for it. The guy was a big asshole, but he wasn't the cause of all my troubles. I was. I never felt bad for myself, never asked God 'why me?' Heck, I understood the basic fundamentals of human intercourse, I knew why I was in the predicament I was in.

Andy Capp had nothing to do with it. He was just in the wrong place at the wrong time and made the mistake of opening his fat mouth.

So, Capp, if this story ever finds its way into your hands, well, I just want to apologize for swatting you across the chops with the Powerstick. Sorry, dude.

"It came alive in my hands, there's some sort of raw power in it."

We crossed the old railroad tracks and Richmond fell behind us.

Adam held the stick with both hands and swung it back and forth like a sword.

"Can you feel it?"

He swung it a couple more times. "Nuh," he said. "Just feels like a stick, really."

"That's no ordinary stick. I'm telling you, it came to life in my own two hands, then it sent a 240-pound lug head straight up in the air. Hell, you seen it."

"Yeah, I did. You got him good."

"No, I just closed my eyes and swung. That stick, I swear, it went for the boy's kisser all on its own."

"She's got one powerful kiss. Laid Cappy flat on his back and had him seeing stars."

"That stick's got a power. I felt it."

"I believe you," he said.

But I don't know if he did or not. Not yet anyway.

"Maybe she only hums with life when you need her. When you're in trouble."

I looked at him and waved him off. "Aw, forget it. Maybe I'm just crazy."

"You're not crazy, Jill."

My feet started to hurt me a mile outside of Richmond. My knees ached too and it was getting downright cold.

"How you feeling?"

"My feet hurt," he said. "You?"

"Yeah. Mine too. I'm a little chilly."

"Here. Take the jacket for a while."

It felt good to pull my old leather on my back. "15 from Berea to Richmond."

"Yeah. Richmond's 3 miles long."

"We've walked 1 mile since."

"'Bout 20 down," Adam figured.

"'Bout 45 to go," I reckoned.

"Damn. Whose idea was this anyway?"

"Yours."

His brow knotted. "Was it?"

"Yep."

"Well, why the hell didn't you talk me out of it?"

"Cause I'm just as stupid as you."

"Yeah. That's probably why we get along so good."

"Probably."

We walked in silence for a little bit. The night was cold and clear and our breath billowed out of our mouths like cigarette smoke. The moon was nice and fat and hung low in the sky. The cicadas buzzed from the trees and something squeaked.

And squeaked.

And squeaked.

And squeaked.

"Is that you?"

He shook his head. "Nuh. I didn't fart."

"No, man, listen."

Squeak.

Squeak.

Squeak.

"That is you."

"What?"

"That squeaking."

We fell silent. Every other step he took was dotted with a squeak.

"You sure that's me?"

I put my hand squarely on his chest. "Stop." I walked on five paces and waved him. "Come on."

Adam came, followed by that squeak, squeak, squeak.

"That's you and your ESPN boots."

"Try to ignore it."

"Awright."

But that squeak was like a dripping faucet in the deep throat of midnight. I couldn't ignore it. It became the only sound in the world and it was driving me absolutely batshit crazy.

"I'm gonna kill you on this dark road, Adam."

"You could use a drink. Let's have a pop."

So the both of us sat down on the gravel shoulder and guzzled a can of Green Lightning.

"You're not coming back next semester, are you?" Adam had his arms propped on his knees. He looked at his soda can instead of me.

"Nuh. I gotta go home. I can't rely on Brian. This is something I'm just not strong enough to do on my own." I was awful glad he was finding that soda can so interesting.

"I'm gonna miss you." His voice was so hollow it made my gut ache.

Things got quiet for a while. Even the cicadas honored us with a moment of silence.

"My legs're cramping up." He finally said, climbing to his feet.

Me, Adam, and the squeak kept heading for faraway Mount Sterling.

8

My dad was a proud union man. He had a big union jacket that he wore out to all the different construction sites he worked on. It had a big, sorta medieval code of arms logo on the back with LOCAL 439 stamped at its heart.

He did electrical work. He stood up on a ladder and soldered wires. When I was a kid, I thought my dad could've gotten called up on some dangerous secret agent assignment, if he just would've sent in his resume. The spy business always needed a brave man who knew to pull the red wire instead of the yellow or blue.

My dad taught me so many things. He taught me how to figure Manny Trio's batting average, taught me to never cook vegetable soup on high, taught me to be honest, to work hard, and to always thank God at the end of the day.

But there are two things he taught me that I keep separate from all the rest. I treasure them like golden nuggets. I keep them in my heart so they'll always be with me no matter where life takes me, high or low, I'll always know the right way to live:

Ten years ago, I had this great mutt named Pook. One day Pook went chasing after my softball. She chased it into the road and got herself tangled up pretty bad, under the wheels of a long, gray Buick.

My dad and me got her to the vet as soon as we could. I carried that dog in my arms and I could feel her poor heart pounding hard and scared against me.

The doc had Pook in the back for a while; Me and dad just sat in the waiting room together, not saying anything. I stared at my hands mostly, watching Pook's blood dry on my fingers, making every little line, every tiny print, a sad little work of art.

The doc stepped into the room. By the look on his face I knew he didn't have good news.

"Pook's busted up pretty bad." He said. "Couple of broken ribs. A deflated lung. Her hind legs're…" He shook his bald head and pushed his glasses up his long nose. "Well, if she makes it, she'll never walk again."

I had to made a decision. It was the first big decision of my life. I wanted to save my dog because I didn't want to lose my best friend. But if the old doc could save Pook, she'd never chase another softball again.

My dad told me, "Jill, this is your dog. So this is your decision. Life's mostly easy choices. But once in a while a big, ugly son of a bitch'll knock you on your ass. And you gotta pray. Pray that God puts the right choice in your heart. And once you make that decision, go with it. Don't ever look back and wish for the moment again."

I let the doc put Pook out of her misery that night. Then I prayed to God that he would take care of my good friend wherever she was now.

9

In the darkness of the night, farmland laid all around us. The land flowed over the hillsides and rolled down into the valleys. There was no noise, save for the cicadas; the squeak; and the wooden pop of the Powerstick meeting the long, lonely road.

Me and Adam didn't talk. We just walked and walked and walked. Walked until, out of the stillness, lunged a great black beast. Its sharp barks cut the quiet night into ribbon tatters. The beast hurled its body at us, but a massive steel chain snapped taunt and jerked the predator, muzzle snarling, jaws gnashing, back to the base of the giant oak tree.

Adam danced wild like a marionette, spun on his toes, and took off the other way. I stood frozen, my heart pounding in my ears, waiting for the savage to charge out of the darkness and pounce on my throat.

The great monster snarled down on us from atop a hill. Her silhouette was black against the fat white moon. She was thick and muscled, built like an ox with the head of a horse. But she was shackled, I could see, chained prisoner to an old reliable oak.

"Adam! Wait!" I shouted, my eyes glued to the beast.

Adam's footsteps still pounded the road, running away from me.

I turned, cupped my hands to my mouth and yelled after him, "AAAAAAAAAdam!"

I couldn't see him anymore, but I couldn't hear him running anymore either.

"It's awright," I called. "She's chained up."

He stepped out of the shadows and into the soft moonlight. "Is she big?" The gnarled tree hid the raging truth from him.

I shook my head, "No."

The dog snapped a volley of vicious barks down the hill at me, calling me a liar.

I cut my hand through the air at my knees. "Bout knee high."

Adam didn't budge. "I got this thing with dogs," he told me. "I can't go any further than this."

"But we got to pass it."

He shook his head. "No, we don't."

"You're scared of that little mutt?"

The dog barked some mean f-yous down the hill and swore about the nasty things she'd do to me if she broke free.

Adam was itching to make tracks, but he swallowed his dry golf ball of fear and held his ground. "Anything that has the potential to chew my throat out, yes, I fear."

"You got the Powerstick. If she comes after you, just beat her down."

"You take the stick." The stick came cartwheeling my direction. It bounded up and off the road, end over end, and clattered at my feet. "You beat her down. But I ain't going."

"Adam." I drew a patient breath. "Look, this road's the only road that goes straight through. I'm not backtracking because you're scared of a little mutt."

The dog let loose on that one, barking and growling herself hoarse. She fought her restraints so fiercely I could hear the spittle gurgle in her throat as the chain choked her. She was really starting to get on my nerves.

"Shut up!" I shouted up the hill. "Nobody asked you!"

"Aw, that's smart. Piss her off. No way I'm going down that road now. She's got a personal vendetta she wants to settle."

I threw my hands in the air. "You want to walk all the way back down that road and find another way?"

"No. But I want to live."

The dog kept on barking. It sounded raw, like it hurt.

"This is crazy." Then I thought about all the farmland that rolled like oceans on both sides of us. "Come on." I said and picked up the Powerstick.

"What?"

I walked off the road, towards an old country fence.

"Where you going?"

I put my hands on the wooden post and tossed one leg over. "I got a plan." I fell to the other side.

"Aw nuts." Adam mumbled, but he followed me to the ocean's edge and he, too, fell in.

The pasture reeked thick of manure. It was the kind of thick reek that wraps its rotten coils around your throat and suffocates every last gasp of pure air clean out of your lungs.

"God damn." I swore and pulled my jacket over my face. "It smells like shit."

"If shit didn't smell like shit we'd call it peppermint."

I blinked at Adam and considered his philosophy for a moment, then reasoned it best to change the subject.

"Here's the plan. We go through this field. We'll come up on the other side, twenty years past the pooch. Meet with your approval?"

He gave me the thumbs up.

So we started off, creeping low through the field, all the while I prayed that God would watch over me. I prayed he'd keep my feet from stumbling off the path of righteousness and into, well, a big pile of shit. Unfortunately, I forgot to pray for Adam.

10

The year my dad died, before he lost all his weight and his hair, before cancer made him a warm, dead body that could blink, my dad gave me that second golden nugget that I keep in my heart:

It was my senior year in high school. Way back then, I was still a virgin, holding onto to my purity until one day I'd meet and fall in love with a man my dad would approve. I wasn't into men. I had my dad. He was the only man I needed. All I wanted to do was make him proud.

Softball was the best way I knew how. I was getting letters from colleges all over the place. Jill, come play here, Jill, come play there. Me and my dad had sorted through most all the letters that buried the kitchen table. We had even gone out to a couple of the schools, to poke around the campuses and just check the joints out.

So boys never really figured into my plans. I wasn't out to catch their attention. All I was interested in catching were line drives and baserunners stealing.

But then the test results came back positive. My dad had a malignant tumor throbbing inside his left lung like a living wasp nest. It was cancer. And it was spreading fast.

I played ball harder than ever my last season. The sicker my dad became, the stronger my game got. My arm was a missile launcher hurling heat seekers across the diamond. My eye sight got so sharp, I swear I could actually admire the seam of the softball writhe like a snake, as the blurring pitch tailed toward me at sixty miles an hour. My bat was fatter than a rowing oar and I swatted base hits through every defense that stood against me.

I was a good player that got great, no lie. And it all had something to do with my dad dying every day. If softball had been the cure for cancer, the way I played that year would've had my dad up on his feet and twenty years younger to boot.

The night we were to play for the state title I went and saw my dad in North Penn Hospital. He had been bed ridden here for two weeks now and had missed my last four games.

He didn't get to see me steal home against Central or turn an unassisted triple play at Catholic or knock in eight runs over in Hazelton. And he missed the bullet I threw, from way down behind third, to beat the fastest chick in the county and Bricktown in the semis. Man, was that some throw. I sure wish he could've seen that one.

He was lying in bed just staring at the ceiling. He had ugly tubes running up his nose and out his arms.

"Dad."

His eyes fought to find me. It took all his strength for him to smile. I sat down next to him and we just looked at each other for a long time.

I never wanted for anything in my life up to that point. My dad had worked hard and made sure of that. But that night, with his tired hand holding mine, I wanted for something he could never give me. I wanted him to live forever.

"Jill," he whispered. "I'm so proud of you."

I didn't want him to say that, because it made it okay for him to slip away from me. I had made him proud—I had done what I was supposed to do. And he had loved and taught me well—his end of the bargain was done too.

The tears fell from my eyes. "I'm so scared, Dad. It's gonna be so tough without you." I thought I meant not having him there that night at the state championship, but my dad, like always, knew the truth. I was talking about the rest of my life.

"You'll be all right, Jill. Just remember, you're the daughter of a rugged construction worker. So you and God, you can get through anything."

That night, in the bottom half of the last inning, I hit the first and only home run of my entire career. It was a shot that spun high above the lights and soared clear over the left field fence. We beat Cherry Hill 5–4 and won the state crown. But I went home that night, locked myself in my room, and cried over the most painful loss of my life.

11

We moved with all the stealth and agility of stand up vacuum cleaners. Two black, arthritic figures stumbling against a giant, purple sky.

I stopped dead. For under the light of the moon, a foot off the ground, running silver and ugly for as far as the eye could see, was an electrical, wire fence.

I put my arm against Adam. "Whoah. Watch yourself. Wire fence."

He looked at it and scratched his beard. "You think it's juiced?"

I shrugged. "Touch it."

He frowned. "You touch it."

"Not with your hand, silly." I offered the Powerstick. "Use this."

"If this fence has got any bite in her, the Powerstick's not gonna tell us about it. Wood doesn't conduct electricity."

I was no scientist. My knowledge of electricity went only as deep as Ben Franklin, a kite, and a key. My dad had taught me a lot about the walk of life, but he didn't teach me to follow in his footsteps.

"Awright." I said. "Piss on it, then."

"Hell no!"

"Piss is conductive."

"Too damn conductive! My cousin took a squirt on an electrical fence once and this blue current surged up his piss stream in a heartbeat. Shocked his pecker and singed his curlies."

"For real?"

"I wouldn't lie about the truth."

"Dammit. Come on, then." I started backtracking through the shit-reeking field madder than all hell on judgment day. We would come up right back where we had started, on the business end of a loaded rotweiler.

I had gotten ahead of Adam, so I didn't notice it when he stopped and stood dumb in the middle of the field. It wasn't until he cleared his throat and said, "Bullshit" that I paid him any mind.

I turned around and blinked at him. "What? Will you come on?"

"Bullshit."

"What's wrong with you?"

"Bull." He said it real slow like he was talking to an idiot. "Shit."

I came toward him, "What do you mean?"

But then I saw. At his feet, coiled and steaming like gutted intestines, was a fat pile of bullshit.

"Oh. You think there's any bulls out here now?" I looked up at him and found his face whiter than a dead Klansman and I knew that there was.

"There's one right behind me, isn't there?"

Adam gulped and nodded.

The only muscles I moved were in my neck, I had to see what we were up against, every other fiber in my body was scared stiff.

Now, I'll admit I'm no bull expert or nothing, but this mammoth beast could've whooped any elephant's ass and had every last blue whale calling him king.

"I'm for damn sure he ain't chained up."

"Bulls," I whispered. "They're just boy cows, right?"

"Yeah. So?"

"Well, maybe he's sleeping, like the cows do."

The bull king just stood there, breathing hard and heavy through its mighty nostrils.

"You think so?" Adam asked.

Truth be known, I was trying not to think. What if this bull king had come to chew cud and kick ass and was all out of cud? "I really hope so."

"We gotta make a move."

I snatched Adam's arm. "No. If he's not asleep, he'll charge."

"True. But it'd be a damn shame if he is asleep and we stand here till morning. He'll wake up and charge us then."

I hated it when Adam made more sense than me. "You're right. Hold on." I started to pull the jacket off.

"What're you doing?"

"If he charges, I'll shake the jacket like a matador."

"Good thinking. You all set?"

"Like the dinner table."

"Let's get outta here."

Now, with an 800-pound bull standing ten yards away, my idea of "Let's get out of here" was turn and run like hell. But Adam was always playing it smarter than me. He grabbed me by the crook of the arm.

"Hey! Take baby steps," he hissed. "You want to get us killed? Two idiots baby stepping through a bull field are less at risk than two idiots running like crazy hell."

I looked at Adam, the massive bull king, then Adam. Although I was confident I could construct a damn solid argument on the merits of running like crazy hell, now was not the time to debate.

"Awright, awright."

We baby stepped backwards, painfully slow and ridiculously careful.

"He's not moving," I muttered.

"What're you trying to jinx us?"

"I didn't know you were so superstitious."

"I'm not," Adam said. "I just got crap luck. Million to one shot of catching some jungle disease, I'd get it. Odds on hitting the Superjack're one in one and a half, forget it. Prize patrol's rolling up to the guy next door."

Right on cue, the beast awoke. The bull king snorted like a train engine and stamped his iron hoof hard into the earth.

"Aw, great," Adam whimpered.

And for a moment the three of us, me, Adam, and the bull king, we stood motionless in time, waiting for someone to make the first move. I guess the bull king thought since he was the biggest, he should be the one to determine the chain of events, cause he swung his head low, the thick twists of his horns aimed straight at our hearts and he charged us full throttle.

"Run!" Adam shouted, but I was long gone all ready.

I forgot about the hot throb in my legs and the sharp pain in my feet. I forgot about the rest of my life and the faith in my God. There was only one thing that mattered to me at that moment and that was that old country fence. I threw myself over it and landed hard on my back.

The world went still. There was no sound, except the beating of my own heart in my ears. I saw hundreds of white dots glimmering on a black canvas. Then everything came back slow. I was looking up at the stars. Streams of white smoke came pouring down on my face and I could hear the heavy breathing of the bull king through giant, leathery lungs.

My eyes rolled backwards and there it was, looming over me like the devil ready to devour my soul. His eyes burned demon red, sweat glistened his barrel chest and he pounded the earth with his heavy foot.

I was safe on the other side of the fence and he knew it. The bull king gave a final, angry snort and then stalked back into the night, tail switching. The darkness welcomed him home and he was gone.

I sat up and looked for Adam. He was in the road on his knees, scraping the sole of one hiking boot on the asphalt. I got up and stumbled to him.

"What're you doing?"

"Stepped in bullshit," he said, not looking up from his task.

"Oh." I sat down next to him and watched as the chunky, wet smears of shit clung to the street. It stunk pretty fierce, enough to make my gut do a dolphin roll, but I was too exhausted to comment. I just laid back and looked up at all the stars and tried breathing mostly through my mouth.

"Cost my mom a hundred and something," Adam muttered as he slapped the sole onto the concrete. "Professionals wear these."

"Adam, stop."

He kept smacking the boot to the street.

"Adam!"

He peeked over his shoulder at me. "Huh?"

"Lay back, man."

Adam looked quizzically at the bottom of his boot. Then he dropped it and laid back next to me. I gave him half my jacket and we shared it like a blanket.

"What're we gonna do?" I sighed. "We got Cujo licking her chops that way and Raging Bull digging in behind us."

"Nothing we can do except wait."

"Wait? That's our plan?"

"Patience ain't a plan, Jill. It's a virtue."

"Oh." We fell silent and just looked up at all them stars for a while.

It was weird laying up that close to Adam. The only times I had ever laid close to a man was with Brian, after he had rolled off me sweaty from sex. And even then, we didn't lay there together, aware of each other. He'd click on some Frankenstein movie or just turn his back to me and fall asleep.

It was a nice weird, though. Just the two of us laying underneath my jacket, sharing body heat and a beautiful big sky. Huh, maybe it was weird because it was so genuine.

"Hey, Adam?"

"Huh?"

"If neither of us is married in say, twenty years, how 'bout we find each other and, you know, tie the knot?"

He rolled his head to look at me. "Are you proposing?"

"No," I said. "Well, kinda, I guess."

"Awright," he said.

And we both looked back up at the stars, content to be right where we were. Nowhere, together.

12

It was finals week and every student on campus was chasing handfuls of No Doz with cups of black coffee and pulling all nighters. The computer center was a madhouse. Every terminal had somebody sweating over it. The waste baskets were overflowing with dead term paper drafts and bookbag zippers were going off all over the room like firecrackers. Everybody was running late for something, it seemed, or had their noses buried in a text book with a fat highlighter clenched between their teeth.

But I wasn't a part of all this lunacy. I would've liked to have been, but my worries were different at the close of that semester. I dealt with my thesis sentences and essay exams without all the anxiety. I just did them and that was that. For me, this was my final week and I was very lonely and reflective. I chewed my cafeteria food slower and took my sweet old time walking to classes. I made a conscious effort to savor my last days at Berea and found myself missing her before I was even gone.

Adam and me had arranged to hang out one last time before life sent us away in different directions. He had a big art project due the next morning, so he packed his thermos of Maxwell House and his caffeine pills in his bag and spent the night in the Arts Building, working on his final painting.

He had left the back door propped open for me. I went inside and up the tight, dark stairwell, to the third floor. The loft was dim and empty. Wooden easels stood like skeletons and their shadows fell long across the floor. Everything was so quiet and still. The crazy life outside had passed it by and left it all alone. I felt very much at peace here.

I saw Adam at the far end. He stood before an easel, his back to me, with a long paint brush in one hand and a wooden palate in the other. I walked passed all the empty easels to his.

"Hey," I said.

He turned and blinked at me, like he was lost someplace else in his mind and trying to get his bearings on the present. It took him a full second, but he grinned at me. Then he stepped to one side and asked, "What do you think?"

The painting was of us, laying there on the side of the dark road, under my leather jacket and the giant sky. It was the most beautiful painting I had ever seen, not for its artistic merits—Adam was a damn good painter, that's all I knew about merits—but for its heart. For what it stood for. Tears were in my eyes and my throat got all tight on itself.

Adam had to ask me again. "So, what do you think?"

"It's good," I whispered. "It's real good."

"It's kind of a tribute." He dropped his brush into a cup of dirty rinse water and sat down on a stool. We looked at each other. "Tribute to me and you and that walk. Goddamn that was a long walk, wasn't it?"

I laughed. "Yeah. It sure was."

And we looked at each other some more. That walk was only two weeks old, but we talked about it like it had happened back in the good old days. I think we knew a lot of time laid between that night and the next time we'd see each other again.

"Jill, look. A lot's gonna happen to me during the next twenty years. But if, you know, that whole marriage thing don't, I'll take one look at this painting and I'll be on a bus around the world looking to find your ass."

The tears were making him blurry. "You promise me?"

"Hell, yeah," he said. "I promise you that."

13

"You hear that?" I sat up and tilted my head.

"Hear what?"

"Sssshhh." I got up.

The low, throbbing pulse of a stereo pumped the night. Over the hill, two headlights blazed through the darkness. The loud rumble of a hot engine chased after the bass.

Adam sat up with my jacket draped over his head. "Thank the sweet Lord Jesus, we're saved."

"You want me to handle this?"

He looked up at me and shrugged. "You're already up. You might as well."

I walked out to the middle of the road and waved my hands over my head at the approaching car. It rolled to a slow stop ten yards off me. The music was pumping so deep and hard my liver started jigging in sync to its rhythm.

I stood there staring at that car, waiting for a signal. That car just growled idle, swaying to its powerful bass beat. I squinted and tried to get a look at the figure behind the wheel, but those headlights were white fire and burned my sights out.

I looked back at Adam.

He shrugged.

I looked back at the car.

The driver could see me, I knew. I could feel the iciness of his stare slide over my flesh, leaving an ugly pucker of goosebumps prickled on every inch. I took a deep breath and walked to the car.

I went directly to the driver's side and found the window had been blown out and replaced with a soiled piece of cardboard duct-taped to the frame. Written in heavy, black marker was:

OTHER SIDE

I cut around the nose of the car and tried to make out the driver through the front window, but the glass had been frosted over in death black. The passenger's side window had been rolled away. I hunkered down and peered inside. Here, the darkness was so complete, so absolute, the glow of my soul's life force started to flicker, suffocating near its nemesis.

"Hey," I said. "Hey" had always been my ice breaker when meeting a stranger.

"How you doing?" This was my hook, line, and sinker. It got no response from the driver.

Standing there, feeling like the world's biggest asshead, I promised myself to work on some slicker material.

Instead I said, "Nice car."

No response.

"What is it? Eighty-nine Reliant?"

Nothing.

"It's not a Reliant, is it?"

Silence.

"That's a shame, cause I hear Reliants are pretty good cars."

Still, all quiet on the western front.

"They got this knack for being, you know, reliable."

There was a sharp click from a Zippo lighter. A blue flame hissed up out of the darkness and licked its hot tongue on the steady end of a Camel. I could see his face for a second, twisted in the flickering blue shadows. He was all cheek bone and scar tissue and then he was gone. Only the red eye of the cigarette burned in the blackness. He took a long drag. Orange ash crawled its way up the smoke.

He had a low, concrete growl. "Greenback."

I just blinked at him, watching the Camel smolder.

"You know where Greenback's at?"

"No, sir."

Silence rose up all around us like flood water. His gloved hand snaked up out of the darkness and pointed through the window at Adam. An icy chill ran up my spine. This was the Grim Reaper and he was choosing his next victim.

"What about your boy? He know where it's at?"

I looked back at Adam, sitting on the side of the road with my jacket over his head, scraping brown wedges of bullshit off his professional hiking boot with the Powerstick. I was about to say no, but then a brilliant light bulb of an idea exploded in my mind.

"Yeah, sure. Adam would know. This is his neck of the woods. He could get you to Greenback blindfolded."

Grim didn't sound impressed. "Oh yeah?"

"Yeah."

He sucked all the life out of that cigarette and exhaled a lungful of poison in my face. "Youse need a ride?"

"We could use a ride."

The dying butt danced in the dark, down away from his face.

"I want to make youse an offer," he said, then flicked the cig at me.

It spun end over end. I ducked out of the window frame. The cig rolled dead in the street behind me and its gasping orange soul winked out. I took a deep breath and stood back up.

"You and your boy get me to Greenback and I'll let youse ride for a while. How's that sound?"

"Cool. Gimme a sec."

I walked back to Adam. He pulled his boot onto his foot and stood up, dusting his hands on his jeans. "So?"

"Adam, I'm about to ask you a simple question and no matter what the truth is, I want you to answer yes."

"Aw, no."

"You know where Greenback Road's at?"

He bit his lip. "Greenback Road, Greenback Road."

"Can you get us there?"

"Nope. Never heard of it."

I pushed him. "I told you to say yes."

"He's looking for Greenback?"

"Yeah. He'll let us ride if we can get him there."

"Well, what if we don't know how to get there?"

"We really didn't see the point in negotiating that option."

We both squinted back at the car. It sat there growling like a mechanical beast, its engine rumbling low and nasty under the hood.

"We need this ride, Jill."

"Yeah. How's your poker face?"

He sighed. "In a dead last tie with my luck."

"Well, way I see it, then, is we got two choices. We bluff." I licked my lips and turned to him. "Or we walk."

Adam thought about it. "Fucket." He said. "Let's do it."

So we hitched a ride with the Grim Reaper. As the Reliant peeled out and tore up the road, I prayed we'd find Greenback before we lost our souls.

14

I never dug my cleats into another batter's box after that championship game. I had offers to play in all kinds of leagues, on all kinds of teams, but I never swung a bat again. I didn't want to. My love for the game died with my dad.

All those college scouts came by the house, wanting to take me out to dinner and explain to me how their systems worked. I just told them no thanks, I had all ready eaten, and then I closed the door on the softball chapter of my life.

A lot of people thought I was crazy. They thought the way I was handling the death of my dad would ruin the rest of my life. But they didn't understand. See, I didn't eat, drink, and dream softball because I loved the game or because I wanted a full ride to some big shot university. I loved softball because I loved being with my dad. It was something we did together. If I ever stepped out on the diamond with him dead, I believe the loneliness that would fill my soul out at shortstop would kill me too.

15

Inside the car the darkness was stifling. I sat in the front, Adam in the back. Grim sat in mystery, hidden in the deep shadows.

"Hey, thanks a lot for the lift." My voice quivered. "We totally appreciate it."

No response.

"Oh, jeez," I laughed. You could smell the nervousness sweating out of my pores. "Where are my manners? My name's Jill, and this here's my good buddy, Adam."

Adam offered his hand over the seat. "How you doing?"

The gloves never relinquished their death grip from the steering wheel. "Jill. Adam." He said. "Which one of you jokers smells like shit?"

"Uh." That "uh" hung in the air until Adam found courage. "That'd be me."

The car screeched to a halt. I went flying into the dash. Adam almost flipped into the front seat. A black glove stabbed an angry finger at us.

"I want that stink outta my ride!"

Adam caught his breath. "But, sir, it's on my boot."

"I'm sick at my stomach! I want it out, now!"

Aw, gosh, I thought. If Adam mentioned the pros on ESPN 2, Grim would reach down our throats and pull out our still beating hearts.

"Adam," I pleaded. "Get rid of the boot."

He blinked at me. "They cost my mom a hundred and something."

"I'm giving you jokers to the count of ten. If I puke before I get there, I'ma mop both your ugly mugs all up in it like country biscuits in gravy. One."

The eyes bugged out of my head. "Adam, lose the boot."

"Two."

Adam just sat there.

"Three."

"You'll have one professional hiking boot left."

"Four."

"Worth fifty bucks, still very impressive."

"Five."

"I love these boots."

"Six."

"They're a pair."

"Adam!" I shouted some sense into him.

"Eight."

"For God's sakes, man, throw the booooooot!"

Adam stripped the boot clean from his foot and cocked it behind his ear, ready to hurl.

"Nine."

"Duck!"

I took cover just as the boot sailed. The engine screamed, and the tires squealed. The car tore up the road like a tiger. We left the boot behind, lying dead in the middle of the road.

I sat in the front seat, next to the Grim Reaper, knee-deep in fear.

"Greenback Road." The voice had a knife-edge to it and it was tracing the flesh of my throat. "We heading in the right direction?"

"Yeah," Adam croaked.

"How far out?"

There followed a pause so ugly even its own mama wouldn't of claimed it.

"I said, how far out?"

Adam rambled. "Not too far. We're pretty close."

"This the same pretty close we were twenty minutes ago?"

"Nuh," Adam gulped. "We're pretty closer now. Just keep going."

My head started to swirl and my guts got tight. Adam, he had turned pasty white like he had just eaten bad fish.

"Awright," Adam said. "Make this right."

"You sure?" Grim growled.

"Yeah." Adam wiped a shiny slick of sweat off his forehead. "Why wouldn't I be sure?"

"All right, then." Grim leaned the car into the right.

A barn loomed up against the sky.

"Son. Of. A. Bitch!" Grim slammed his foot on the brake.

The tires shrieked. I smacked my head on the glove box and Adam fell on the floor.

"That's the barn we just passed a couple miles back!" Grim pounded his fist into the wheel.

I rubbed the goose egg that was now throbbing on my head and smiled like an ass. He was right, of course, Adam had bluffed his way into a complete circle. But I tried to squeeze a couple more miles out of the lift.

"Nuh," I said, "that's how Kentucky is. Barnyard after barnyard, it all looks the same."

"It **IS** the same barn!" Grim swore.

I shook my head, "No it ain't."

He pounced out of the dark at me. His face snarled an inch above mine. His eyes glowed milky white and the corners of his mouth were spiked with long, sharp fangs.

"Yes. It. Is," he hissed. His breath was a hot cloud of fire and brimstone. "Get out before I eat your lying throats."

Adam and me scrambled out of that car fast. I hugged the hard asphalt tight. Grim left us there, lying scared in an oily fog of exhaust. The Reliant flew up the road like a bat out of hell, the tail lights grew smaller and smaller and the screaming engine more distant.

"You awright?"

I rolled over and looked at Adam.

"Yeah," I said. "You?"

"I'm standing here." He held his hand out to me.

I took it and he helped me to my feet. We stood there, in the middle of the road, with miles of dark nothingness rolling on all sides.

"Well," he said.

"Well," I said.

"We made 10 miles."

"We lost a boot."

We both looked at his feet. One professional hiking boot. One dirty sock. He wriggled his toes.

"Was it the one that squeaks?"

He shrugged. "I dunno."

Then he took a little test walk.
Squeak. Squeak. Squeak.
Adam shook his head. "Nope."

16

There were now three of us staggering towards Mount Sterling. Me, Adam, and Misery. Misery didn't complain and her boot didn't squeak, but she was still a God awful pain in the ass.

My feet were fat, throbbing hunks of flesh that threatened to split open and bleed hot agony. My knees kept on popping, my back was stiff as hell, and my shoulders ached something fierce. If I hadn't been so damn stubborn I would of been happy to just lay down and die. Instead, I kept picking them up and putting them down.

Because, far out there, flashing yellow hope, was a traffic light. It was a beacon that.

    Called.
     To.
      Us.

That flashing light gave me a reason to drag my sorry soul onward and it gave me a hope that if I kept going, soon I would stumble out of the darkness and into the light.

"We're never going to make it." Adam was moving his lips, but Misery was doing the talking. "That light's an evil mirage, grinning out there on a horizon that don't exist."

We staggered on for ten paces. Adam's sock bottom whispered itself thin on the asphalt.

"Every step we take, it just floats out there. It ain't getting any closer."

I didn't say anything. I just kept on walking and fought to keep my chin up and my eyes on that far away light.

"I gotta piss like a champ."

The Green Lightning was knocking on my door too, but having to piss kept me moving and moving was the only thing that kept me from dying.

"My sock's wet," Adam sniffed. "I think a blister just popped."

The more Adam talked the more I wanted to just curl up on the side of the road and cry my eyeballs out of my head. So I started to hum.

The tune was a part of me that I didn't know about. It came to me without thought, like a survival instinct. I knew the tune, because I was humming it like I had been humming it ever since I was a buck-toothed kid, but I didn't know where it came from.

Adam recognized the tune too, and he started humming right along with me. I clapped my hands to our rhythm and Adam popped the Powerstick on the road, keeping time with each weary step. And then it hit me.

It was the campfire song from *Glory*. The same song the Massachutes 54th sung before they went into battle, willing to die for their freedom. Only our lyrics went something like this here:

"Lordy, oh, Lordy." Adam threw his head back while I kept on humming and clapping.

> *"This road ahead lies mighty long.*
> *To get to the end, we gots to be strong!*
> *With the Powerstick in one hand—"*

He double popped the Powerstick on that line, and by the way Adam's tired step became a lively stride, I believe that stick had started humming again too.

> *"—And nothing in the other,*
> *I'll look out for my sister,*
> *And she, her brother."*

Both of us slung our arms around each other and belted out the chorus:

> *"Whoah, my Lord, Lord, Lord, Lord.*
> *Whoah, my Lord, Lord, Lord, Lord.*
> *Ummmm-Hmmmm.*
> *Ummmm-Hmmmm."*

"Your turn, girl."

"Nuh," I smiled, playing shy. "I couldn't do it as good as you."

He threw his arms in the air. "Come on now, child. Let Jeeeeeeesus know you love him! Let Jeeeeeesus know you need him!"

So I shouted "Lord!" up to Him to make sure I got his attention. Then I sang.

> *"Me and my boy here,*
> *We got a lot of pride.*
> *But now, oh Lord,*
> *There's a heap of pain a coming*
> *With each and every stride."*

"Go on now, sister."

> *"See, Lord, we feeling low,*
> *And we feeling beat,*
> *So we's asking you,"*

"Uh-huh."

> *"To carry us through."*

"That's right."

> *"And to keep us both—"*

"Bring it home, girl."

> *"On our feet!"*

As we rolled into the chorus again, that light didn't seem so damn far off.

> *"Whoah, my Lord, Lord, Lord, Lord.*
> *Whoah, my Lord, Lord, Lord, Lord.*
> *Ummmm-Hmmmm.*
> *Ummmm-Hmmmm."*

For the next five hundred yards, we were invincible.

17

I meant what I said to Adam back there with all my soul. I would've married him right then under my jacket if he would've asked me to. And I would marry Adam to this day if ever he offered me the chance, no matter what my grandmother had to say about it.

"Jill, you don't want no southern boy. They're nothing but racist rednecks deep down in their heart of hearts."

See, Adam was always good to me. He looked me honest in the eye and knew how to listen. He never once judged me. With Adam, he never pointed out my mistakes. He only helped me try to fix them.

There was a drawback to the boy, though. He was a shamefully lazy guy. He'd spend more time complaining about his job than he would working it. If God ever stuck the two of us together till death did us part, I would have to be the main bread winner of our family.

But you know, for a guy as honest and true as Adam, I would work my fingers to the bone and every bone to the knuckle, if I had to.

I've only loved two men my whole life.
Adam was one.

18

"I hate that light," Adam sneered. "I've never hated anything more than the way I'm hating that light."

"Keep picking them up and putting them down. We'll get there."

"Yeah. My mom's gonna kill me when we get there."

"No mom's gonna kill her only son for braving 65 miles to come home to see her."

"No," Adam agreed. "She'll kill me because she's the mother, the world's a dangerous place, and I'll understand it all when I'm a parent."

He kicked a rock with his boot foot. "I don't know anymore. I used to think that Mom, she might not've always agreed with me, but she always believed in me. I don't think like that anymore."

He shrugged. "Somewhere along the line, I disappointed her. And if Dad could still get it up like he could when he was seventeen, I bet she'd try for a brand new son."

"Come on, man, don't say that."

"No, it's true. You know what she said to me when I came home last weekend?"

I shook my head, "What?"

"She told me that I should change my major to something more practical. Something I could get a real job with."

"Ouch. That hurts."

"Hurts bad. I said, Ma, don't you appreciate my art? Don't you believe I can make it as a painter?"

"And she said?"

"Of course I appreciate your art, Adam. I'm your mother."

I laughed.

"In her mind, I'm going to college to make pretty things to hang on her refrigerator."

"Well, why are you going?"

He got quiet all of a sudden. "I don't know," he said with half the steam. "Where else am I supposed to go? Huh? Mop a toilet for five an hour? Get a buzz cut and salute the flag? I don't know. What about you?"

I shrugged.

"You don't have an opinion? I can't believe that."

"What do you want me to say?"

"Say something."

"Well, I'm not going to say everything's gonna be all right, that's for damn sure. I don't believe in that anymore. All I know for sure is that I'm young and I'm stupid. I had a world of opportunity and now I'm dropping out to have a baby. So if you're asking me for advice, Adam, all I got for you is ask somebody else for it and then thank God that you ain't me."

I was looking straight at him, but he was being real careful not to look at me. The flashing yellow light bathed his face in soft yellow, then he fell pale and white, then yellow again.

"You're standing waist deep in opportunity, Adam. You owe it to yourself to wake up and work hard. Don't mess it all up like I did."

19

On the second day I was at Berea College, the entire freshman class was required to report to an orientation assembly. So all four hundred of us packed into the rickety auditorium and suffered through boring speeches made by dangerously old men.

The only thing I truly remember from that long afternoon in the hot guts of Danforth Chapel was what a guy named John McFee said. He was a proud, old alumnus from the 1847 goldrush or something. He wore wire-rim specs and had a map of liverspots stained on his bald head.

His tired voice quivered into the whining microphone. "I want everybody to turn and look at the person on your left," he said. "Now turn and look at the person on your right. Four years from today, when you walk up on this stage to shake President Shinn's hand and accept your degree, these fellow classmates will not be there."

He let that uncomfortable fact dry up on us like dead skin. Then he said, "Berea is a long journey. Only the strong will finish this journey."

My whole life, up until that walk, I had been a starter, not a finisher. I had lost touch with summer camp friends because I never got around to mailing their letters. I had a stack of books sitting on the shelf with my pages ear marked, but their stories long forgotten. I had kept a diary for a month straight before I kicked it under my bed. I had read the Bible every day for two weeks, but never got a verse past Leviticus 3. Hell, I was even bulimic for a while. I made for a damn good binger, but I lacked the dedication to purge and ended up fifteen pounds heavier than when I started.

That night, in the middle of God forsaken nowhere, with the lights of Richmond fading behind us and the city of Winchester blazing ahead, I swore things would be different.

If I sunk to my knees and gave up, I would wish to be back on that long, dark road every single day of my life. I swore right then and there that I would keep on walking through my loneliness, keep on going despite the pain. I would walk until the world ran out of road.

20

"I could knock that son of a bitch out with a softball from here." I couldn't help but grin. We were going to do it. We were going to beat that light. It was only a long throw from left field away.

Adam laughed. "How you feeling?"

"Born again."

"Oh yeah?"

"Yeah."

Adam turned to me. "Hey?"

"Huh?"

And then he was off running, calling over his shoulder, "Race ya!"

I took off hard after him. The two of us ran awkward and ugly like ostriches. The hard asphalt sent aching splinters of pain up my legs, but it was a beautiful pain. The kind of pain you're proud of, like a battle scar. It was pain that said I had suffered, I had struggled, but I had refused to quit.

And now, as me and Adam threw our weary bodies to our knees under the traffic light and raised our hands triumphantly towards the sky, that pain was real, like the hope that flashed yellow all around us.

21

The Red Lion Diner was a rundown little joint. There were three pick-up trucks sitting in the dirt lot. It was the hard dirt that crunched under your shoes. The windows were spotted with dead gnats and dust.

Adam got to the door first and held it open. He curtsied me past with a regal wave of his hand and a slight nod.

"After you, my lady."

The boy might've been drop ass tired, but his mama sure did raise him right.

Inside was dim, every light in the place was humming on its last watt. We stood by the old cash register and waited. Around the bend came a mean looking dude. He had a fat, bald head with a full beard of red fire. He wore a tight white tee shirt and jeans that bled blue. His forearms were knotty and covered with ancient, mysterious tattoos of serpents, dragons, devils, and Tweety Bird.

He eyed us hard and spit a neat jet of tobacco juice behind the counter.

"There's a four dollar minimum per person after midnight. Means ya'll's bill's gotta mount to least eight dollars. Ain't no exceptions to this here policy. Ya'll still interested in a table?"

"No," I said.

"Didn't think so." The man started to turn away.

But I called him back. "You got bathrooms?"

He raised one bushy brow and considered my question. "Only got one john in operation tonight. Shame for you it's the men's john." He pulled his lips into a ragged, raw grin.

"I'd like to use your men's room, then, sir."

The tight muscles in his face twitched. "But you ain't no man."

"No," I said. "No, I'm not."

His gray eyes cut from me to Adam. He pointed a crooked finger at Adam's feet. One professional hiking boot, one filthy sock.

"Shirt and SHOES're required in my establishment, son. Or can't you read the sign out front?"

"Look, mister, we don't want no trouble," Adam said. "We just want to piss and die."

The man put his hands on his wide hips and spit another stream of dark juice behind the counter. He looked at us hard. "Awright, but be quick about the business and don't do your dying on my property."

"No, sir, we won't," I promised.

He thumbed over his shoulder to an old man hunkered over a cup of coffee and a rifle magazine. "Swing a left at Harold, then go straight back."

"Thank you," Adam said, then he turned to me and smiled. "Ladies first."

If I didn't have to piss so bad, I wouldn't of used the awful stick hole in the Red Lion Diner. It was a tight place with hissing pipes and a leaking sink. There was one urinal rotting on the far wall. There was one shattered mirror hanging on a rusted nail. There was one toilet. No seat. Brown sludge burped in its throat and I swear something was moving in that bowl.

When it was Adam's turn, he hobbled off toward Harold, favoring his right leg real bad. I watched him limp around the corner, then I sat down on the floor and waited. I let my eyes slip closed and my bones soak up the heat.

I heard the manager say, "Hey, Miss", but I didn't think he was talking to me. Why would he be? I was out of the way, minding my own business, not bothering a single soul.

He cleared his throat and said louder and sharper than the last time, "Hey, Miss."

I raised my weary head and squinted at him.

He loomed over the counter, his giant hands planted on the wooden top. He eyed me long and hard. "Ya'll running from the law?"

I frowned. "No."

"You got any ID?"

"No."

"I'ma have to ask you to wait outside. I can't have no unsavory riffraff loitering in my diner."

Harold staggered to the register just then. His eyeballs were drowning in Wild Turkey and his fly was yawning wide open. Harold handed the manager his bill and a soiled five.

"You sitting in the corner like some dirty Injun's disrespectful to my paying customers."

"I'm just waiting on my friend, sir."

"If you ain't waiting in line to pay your bill, then you ain't waiting in my diner. Now, take your ass outside."

Rage pulled me to my feet. I glared at him, but he just turned away from me like I didn't exist any more.

"Gawdamn kids, Harold. We fought the war for them lowlifes."

Harold belched. "Gawdamn waste."

"My apologies, buddy. That'll be two dollars and seven cents all together."

The exception that had been made for Harold was the final kick in the teeth. I stormed out of the Red Lion Diner and into the chill of the night. I was fuming mad and pacing like a caged panther when Adam came out.

"My foot's bleeding awful bad," he said.

He had walked the last 15 miles in a tube sock. It was stained and stiff with dark red. He had sacrificed and he had suffered. Now, it was my turn.

I sat down and pulled off my Nike. "Here."

He looked at the shoe. "It'll be a tight fit."

"Tight's good for your foot. Pressure'll stop the bleeding."

He didn't buy that logic, but he took the shoe anyway.

He crammed his toes into my sneaker. "I'm not gonna make it."

"You'll make it," I got up. "You got no other choice."

We headed across the lot, towards the interstate. Me with one trusty Nike and one white sock. Adam with one hiking boot and a little piece of me.

22

We made the interstate an hour before dawn. 55 miles down, but the world's longest 10 still stretched between us and the promised land, Mount Sterling.

The interstate was long and dead at a quarter to four in the morning. We staggered along the shoulder for close to a mile before a car even roared on past us. The headlights threw Adam's shadow long in front of me. I could see his arm outstretched, his thumb up, hopeful of flagging down the good Samaritan.

Things were pretty clear to me. It was the two of us against the rest of the world and it was pissing me off, that after all the blues we had sung, Adam still believed in a white knight.

I turned around and looked at him.

"Put your hand in your pocket."

"Somebody'll stop, Jill."

"Nobody gives a damn."

He just shook his head and said what he had said all ready. "Somebody'll stop, Jill."

"No, Adam. It's just me, you, and this long interstate, so get that through your head and keep your legs moving cause that's the only way we're getting home."

He blinked at me with the red, tired eyes of a bloodhound.

"Somebody'll stop, Jill."

And, son of a bitch, somebody did.

It was a big truck with a loud breathing engine, driven by a guy who called himself Potbelly. Potbelly was an old man with an old man's grin I didn't quite trust, but when he threw open the door to his cab and told us to hop on in, why I laughed like I was climbing up into heaven.

"Dat's right, sugar plum, git yer sweet self on in here."

There were two seats like kitchen chairs. I got in first, so I sat between them, on the floor, with the gear shift between my legs. Adam and Potbelly talked, Potbelly mostly. Me, I just sat there becoming one with that truck, letting the floor vibrate all the pain right out of my body.

"So, where ya'll headed?"

"Mount Sterling."

"Be 'bout 12 miles up."

"That sounds right. We really appreciate this lift."

"Hey, no sweat, lil' man. I'm just glad to get myself some good company. So what's yer name, lil' lady?"

"Jill."

"Jewel?"

"Jill. Like Jack and Jill."

"Jill, why dat's a beauful name you got dere, Jill."

That should've been a tip off. There was no beauty to Jill. It was a simple, plain, four letter word with as much eloquence as spit, piss, or poor. But I was too awful tired to be picking up on any clues.

"So what's your story, lil' man? You Jill's Jack?"

"Nuh." Adam's head rattled against the window. "My name's Adam. And we're just friends."

"You don't say." Potbelly whistled. "I reckoned the two of ya'll was setting off to elope."

"Nuh. Just walking home."

"Where ya'll coming from?"

"Berea College."

"Gawddamn, boy! Dat's a solid 40 miles south of here."

"It's a ways if you're walking."

"Ya'll must be dead tired."

"Tired. But we ain't dead."

I must've started to doze, cause everything took on an underwater quality, like I was semi-conscious in someone else's dream. A hand was on my leg. Now, I know that this hand had no business on my leg, but I was just so tired. The thought had registered, but my spider senses weren't tingling.

It wasn't until that hand floated like a phantom and pressed its sweaty palm on my chest that my spider senses started tingling like a mother fucker. It was Potbelly, our good Samaritan, and he was feeling me up hard like my tits were the last two in the county.

I tried to move away, but that cab was just so tight. I was like a mouse trying to hide from a big hand in the corners of a shoebox.

So, I sat there with tears in my eyes and dirty fingers down my shirt, knowing that I was learning a valuable lesson, but knowing too, that sometimes being dumb beats the hell out of getting wise.

"Watching dat white line pass on by's a beauful sight, ain't it, lil' man?"

"You sure got that right," I heard Adam say from a hundred miles away. "You're the best thing that's happened to the two of us all night long."

Potbelly's laugh rotted in his throat. "Shucks, I'm just doing my part like any other decent man would a done. Besides, it ain't like ya'll are the only ones benefiting from dis here relationship. It's symbosis."

His thumbnail flecked my nipple.

"I do fer ya'll by giving ya'll a lift, ya'll do fer me by giving me some companionship on a lonely night."

"Sounds like the perfect trade off," Adam said.

"Oh, lil' man, it is. More than you know."

I sat in silence and traded my dignity for those last 10 miles.

23

It was my last night at Berea College, a rainy night at the tail end of May. All my stuff was packed in duffel bags and a hideous yellow suitcase my aunt picked up at some yard sale.

I sat in the dark, on a stripped naked mattress I used to call my bed. Some other girl would sleep here next semester. Some other girl would hang her clothes in my closet. Some other girl would crack open a book and study at my desk.

I closed my eyes and I hoped for that girl's sake she wouldn't be as stupid as I had been. I hoped she knew that there were always consequences she would have to pay and she could never plead loneliness to get off.

The phone rang.

"Hello?"

"Jill."

I hadn't seen or heard from Brian in a full month, but when I heard his voice on the other end, I could feel his arms around me and hear his heartbeat like we had just made love yesterday.

"Jill," he said again.

I don't know why, really, but I couldn't speak. I was all choked up and my eyes were blurry with tears. Maybe it was the darkness or the solitude or the rain, but more than likely, it was the hope that I hadn't let die. The hope that Bri would come back and stand by me.

"Jill."

"Yeah?" I whispered.

"I'm outside."

My insides started swirling and my heart got so hot I thought it would pop. He was downstairs, on the porch, and he had come to see me.

"I want to talk to you."

The tears ran down my face like the rain on the window. I couldn't hold them back.

"Okay," I whispered.

I hung up the phone and pulled on my faithful leather jacket. Then I went downstairs with my heart in my throat.

I opened the door and stepped out on the long, wooden porch of Fairchild Hall. The rain was falling heavy on the roof. I didn't see Brian at first and my heart almost broke. But then he stepped out of the shadows on the far end.

His shoulders weren't wide and strong anymore, but weary. His eyes were tired and when he spoke to me, I could feel his heart bleeding.

"I been missing you, girl."

I ran to that boy and threw my arms around him. I put my face into his chest and I cried. Looking back, I guess I could've been stronger. I guess I shouldn't have let him off so easy. But if had acted any other way, I wouldn't have been for real.

He held me tight. "Jill."

I turned my face up at him.

He wiped the tears from my cheeks. "I been thinking a whole lot. Bout what we should do. I like you, baby, too much for my own good. If this shit woulda happened five years down the road, it'd be different.

I had no idea what he was talking about. He still held me strong in his arms, but the warmth of his embrace was slipping away. I was losing him. The hurt I had buried deep down in my gut rolled over and woke up again.

I saw my dad putting the science fair trophy on the shelf and I felt the hard corner of second base bite into the arch of my foot as I turned and headed for third.

"I been saving up. I got three hundred bucks. There's a place in Lexington that'll take you up to twelve weeks."

My heart started to beat slow and the blood pulsed like sludge in my ears. The rain. I heard the rain beat down on the long, black casket as they lowered my dad into the ground. I tasted the dirt as I dove hard into home, under the big, swatting mitt of the catcher's tag.

"I made a mistake, baby. I gotta be a man and fix it. I can't deal with a kid now, I'm not ready. I want to marry one woman and I want her to have all my children, baby. I want to do it right. Me and you, Jill, we ain't right."

I saw my dad's chair. Its lonely shadow cast long under the reading lamp, empty. I saw my old leather mitt lying in the dumpster behind the high school, dead.

It was over. I had to let go. I had the rest of my life to live.

I fell away from Brian.

24

"This'll be us coming up." Adam pressed his finger to the glass and pointed to the exit sign that read:

MOUNT STERLING 1

"All ready?"

"Yessir."

Potbelly rumbled his beast off to the shoulder of the road, the brakes hissed, and the oily engine growled idle.

I climbed on out of that truck fast, like the P.A. had announced there was a bomb on board. Adam told me later he had actually apologized for the way I bolted out of there.

"Don't pay her no mind, Potbelly. She don't mean to be rude. She just ain't feeling all that good."

Potbelly grinned with tiny, rotten teeth. "I beg to differ, lil' man. She felt mighty good to me."

Potbelly winked as Adam climbed down.

"Thanks again."

"No, thank you. The pleasure was all mine."

Adam slammed the heavy door shut, then Potbelly drove his truck long down the interstate. The red tail lights disappeared into the predawn and the growl of the truck became a faded echo in the valley.

Adam caught up to me. "That sure was a lucky break, wasn't it?"

He saw the tears in my eyes.

"What's wrong?"

I told him his lucky break wasn't nothing but a pervert trying to cop a feel. He felt sorry for what happened and that made me feel worse.

"Jeez, Jill. I didn't know."

"There wasn't anything you could do. I shoulda known anyway. Nobody just does stuff for nothing. Everybody's got a motive, a trade off."

"Why didn't you say something to me?"

"And lose our ride? No way. We woulda never made it."

That night, exhausted, cold, and wearing my pride down around my ankles, I made a pact with God. I promised Him that I would never be like that. I would go around and just do good for the hell of it.

We staggered down the exit ramp in silence. Adam slipped out of the jacket and wrapped it around my shoulders. He gave me the Powerstick cause I needed it and he put his arm around my waist because I needed him.

I would be all right. After all, I was the daughter of a rugged construction worker. But I leaned on Adam that whole last mile home.

25

So, that's how we went from Berea to Mount Sterling. That was my last college semester. I managed to keep my head on straight and posted three A's and a B. Then I had a baby.

Adam, he held out for one more, before he quit and chased his dream. Last I heard, he was still living with his folks working odd jobs, painting old barns and country fences for the neighbors.

It's been a long time since we talked, going on four years. But life's like that, I guess. After all, friends can't stay in your life forever, no matter how much you love them. Sometimes it gets lonely without them. You miss their smile and their laugh and their hug. But you got to keep on walking. Always keep picking them up and putting them down.

The two of us stood in front of the house. It was smaller than I remembered. Weeds choked the lawn and bird white splotched the roof top. The squad car in the driveway had been replaced with a maroon Oldsmobile.

My leather jacket hung loose on me, the years in between had been lean and hard. I took a deep breath and my insides swirled with the peaceful sadness of lost time.

"Come on, Adam," I said to my beautiful little boy.

He had the old Powerstick clenched tight in one small hand and mine in the other. He looked up at me with the big, brown eyes of his daddy and for a second, my heart ached for the old days that I'd never get back. I smiled at his perfect innocence.

"I want you to meet an old friend of mine," I said.

And together, me and little Adam walked up to the house.

bean dog productions